GOLDILOCKS
and **THE THREE BEARS**

Retold and illustrated by

JAMES MARSHALL

DIAL BOOKS FOR YOUNG READERS • *New York*

• For Trevor Brandon Johnson •

Published by Dial Books for Young Readers
A Division of Penguin Books USA Inc.
375 Hudson Street • New York, New York 10014

Copyright © 1988 by James Marshall
All rights reserved
Printed in the U.S.A.
Typography by Jane Byers Bierhorst

(b)
5 7 9 10 8 6 4

The art for each picture consists of an ink and watercolor painting,
which is color-separated and reproduced in full color.

Library of Congress Cataloging in Publication Data

Marshall, James, 1942–
Goldilocks and the three bears

Summary • Three bears return home from a walk to
find a little girl asleep in baby bear's bed.
[1. Folklore.   2. Bears—Folklore.] I. Three bears.   II. Title.
PZ8.1.M3554Go 1988   398.2'1   [E]   87-32983
ISBN 0-8037-0542-5 • ISBN 0-8037-0543-3 (lib. bdg.)

Once there was
a little girl called Goldilocks.
"What a sweet child,"
said someone new in town.
"That's what *you* think,"
said a neighbor.

One morning Goldilocks's mother
sent her to buy muffins in the next village.
"You must promise *not* to take the shortcut
through the forest," she said.
"I've heard that bears live there."
"I promise," said Goldilocks.
But to tell the truth Goldilocks
was one of those naughty little girls
who do *exactly* as they please.

Meanwhile in a clearing
deeper inside the forest,
in a charming house all their own,
a family of brown bears
was sitting down to breakfast.

"Patooie!" cried big old Papa Bear.
"This porridge is scalding!
  I've burned my tongue!"
"I'm dying!" cried Baby Bear.
"Now really," said Mama Bear,
  who was of medium size.
"That's quite enough."

"I know," said Papa Bear.
"Why don't we go for a spin
 while the porridge is cooling?"
"Excellent," said Mama Bear.
 So they got on their rusty old bicycle
 and off they went.

A few minutes later
Goldilocks arrived
at the bears' house.
She walked right in
without *even* bothering to knock.
On the dining room table
were three inviting bowls
of porridge.
"I don't mind if I do,"
said Goldilocks,
helping herself
to the biggest bowl.

But the porridge in the biggest bowl was much too hot.
"Patooie!" cried Goldilocks.
And she spat it out.
Next she tasted the porridge in the medium-sized bowl.
But that porridge was much too cold.

Then Goldilocks tasted the porridge in the little bowl, and it was *just right*—neither too hot nor too cold.

In fact she liked it so much
that she gobbled it all up.

Feeling full and satisfied Goldilocks thought
it would be great fun to have a look around.
Right away she noticed
a lot of coarse brown fur everywhere.
"They must have kitties," she said.

In the parlor there were three chairs.
"I don't mind if I do," she said,
climbing into the biggest one.
But the biggest chair was much too hard,
and she just couldn't get comfortable.

Next she sat in
the medium-sized chair.
But that chair was much too soft.
(And she thought she might *never* get out of it.)

Then Goldilocks sat in the little chair,
and that was *just right*—
neither too hard nor too soft.
In fact she liked it so much
that she rocked and rocked—
until the chair fell completely to pieces!

Now, all that rocking left
Goldilocks quite tuckered out.
"I could take a little snooze,"
she said.
So she went to look
for a comfy place to nap.
Upstairs were three beds.
"I don't mind if I do," said Goldilocks.
And she got into the biggest one.
But the head of the biggest bed
was much too high.

Next she tried the medium-sized bed.
But the head of that bed was much too low.
Then Goldilocks tried the little bed, and it was *just right*.
Soon she was all nice and cozy and sound asleep.
She did not hear the bears come home.

The three bears were mighty hungry.
But when they went in for breakfast,
they could scarcely believe
their eyes!
"Somebody has been in
my porridge!" said Papa Bear.
"Somebody has been in
my porridge!" said Mama Bear.
"Somebody has been
in my porridge,"
said Baby Bear.
"And eaten it all up!"

In the parlor
the three bears were in
for another little surprise.
"Somebody has been sitting
in my chair!" said Papa Bear.
"Somebody has been sitting
in *my* chair," said Mama Bear.
"Somebody has been sitting
in my chair," said Baby Bear.
"And broken it to smithereens!"

The three bears went upstairs on tiptoe
(not knowing what they would discover).
At first everything seemed fine.
But then Papa Bear lay down on his
big brass bed.
"Somebody has been lying
in my bed!" he cried.
And he was not amused.

"Egads!" cried Mama Bear.
"Somebody has been lying
 in *my* bed!"
"Look!" cried Baby Bear.
"Somebody has been lying in my bed.
 And she's still there!"

"Now see here!" roared Papa Bear.
Goldilocks woke up with a start.
And her eyes nearly popped out of her head.
But before the bears could demand
a proper explanation, Goldilocks was out of bed,

out the window, and on her way home.
"Who *was* that little girl?" asked Baby Bear.
"I have no idea," said Mama Bear.
"But I hope we never see her again."

And they never did.

For my beautiful niece, Alexandra Isabel

Para mi hermosa sobrina, Alexandra Isabel

—M.B.

For Xiryn Bristol Ananta

Para Xiryn Bristol Ananta

—D.D.

The traditional jump rope chant that
appears in the story is in the public domain.

Text copyright © 2015 by Monica Brown
Illustrations copyright © 2015 by David Diaz
Spanish translation copyright © 2015 by Lee & Low Books Inc.
Children's Book Press, an imprint of LEE & LOW BOOKS INC.
95 Madison Avenue, New York, NY 10016. leeandlow.com

Spanish translation by Adriana Domínguez
Book design by Christy Hale
Book production by The Kids at Our House
The text is set in Hypatia Sans Pro Semibold
The illustrations are rendered in mixed media
Manufactured in China by Jade Productions, July 2017
10 9 8 7 6 5 4
First Edition

Library of Congress Cataloging-in-Publication Data
Brown, Monica.
Maya's blanket / story, Monica Brown ; illustrations, David Diaz ; Spanish translation,
Adriana Domínguez = La manta de Maya / cuento, Monica Brown ; ilustraciones, David Diaz ;
traducción al español, Adriana Domínguez. — First edition
pages cm
Inspired by the traditional Yiddish folk song Hob ikh mir a Mantl (I had a little coat)
Summary: "When a little girl's cherished baby blanket becomes old and worn, it is made into a dress,
and over the years it is made into even smaller and smaller items, eventually ending up as a bookmark and
inspiring the creation of a book. Includes an author's note and a glossary" — Provided by publisher.
ISBN 978-0-89239-292-6 (hardcover : alk. paper)
[1. Recycling (Waste)—Fiction. 2. Handicraft—Fiction. 3. Blankets—Fiction. 4. Spanish language
materials—Bilingual.] I. Diaz, David, illustrator. II. Domínguez, Adriana, translator.
III. Title. IV. Title: Manta de Maya.
PZ73.B68565 2015
[E]—dc23
2014029561

Maya's Blanket
LA MANTA DE MAYA

story / cuento **Monica Brown**

illustrations / ilustraciones **David Diaz**

Spanish translation / Traducción al español **Adriana Domínguez**

Children's Book Press, *an imprint of* Lee & Low Books Inc.

New York

Little Maya Morales had a special *manta* that she loved very much. The blanket was blue and green, with purple butterflies that Abuelita had stitched with her own two hands when Maya was just a baby. Maya slept under her *manta* every night, and it kept her cozy and warm. Her *manta* was magical too—it protected her from bad dreams.

But after a while, Maya's *manta* became frayed around the edges.

La pequeña Maya Morales tenía una manta especial que quería mucho. La manta era azul y verde, con unas mariposas moradas que Abuelita le había cosido con sus propias manos cuando Maya era sólo un bebé. Todas las noches, Maya dormía bajo su manta suave y calentita. La manta también era mágica, ya que protegía a Maya de los malos sueños.

Hasta que un día, los bordes de la manta de Maya se empezaron a desgastar.

So with her own two hands and Abuelita's help, Maya made her *manta* into a *vestido* that she loved very much. She wore the dress to her cousin's *quinceañera*. The purple butterflies whirled and swirled as Maya danced with her friends. When Maya twirled so fast that she got dizzy, her magical *vestido* didn't let her fall.

But by accident Maya spilled a glass of red punch on the front of her *vestido*. No matter what she and Abuelita tried, they couldn't get the stain out.

Así que, con sus propias manos y la ayuda de Abuelita, Maya convirtió su manta en un vestido que quería mucho. Maya se puso el vestido para la quinceañera de su prima. Sus mariposas moradas daban vueltas y vueltas cuando Maya bailaba con sus amigos. Aunque Maya dio vueltas tan rápido que se mareó, su vestido mágico no la dejó caer.

Pero por accidente, Maya derramó un gran vaso de ponche rojo sobre el frente de su vestido. Aunque Maya y Abuelita hicieron todo lo que pudieron, no lograron quitar la mancha.

So with her own two hands and Abuelita's help, Maya made her *vestido* that was her *manta* into a *falda* that she loved very much. She wore the skirt to the park, and it bounced as she hopped and skipped rope with her friends. With her magical *falda*, Maya could jump higher than anyone else.

But as Maya grew and stretched toward the sky, her *falda* became too small.

Así que, con sus propias manos y la ayuda de Abuelita, Maya convirtió el vestido que había sido su manta, en una falda que quería mucho. Se la puso para ir al parque, donde se balanceaba mientras Maya brincaba a la cuerda con sus amigos. Con su falda mágica, Maya podía brincar más alto que cualquiera de ellos.

Pero a medida que Maya crecía y se estiraba hacia el cielo, la falda le empezó a quedar pequeña.

So with her own two hands and Abuelita's help, Maya made her *falda* that was her *vestido* that was her *manta* into a *rebozo* that she loved very much. She wore the shawl when she and her friends played games in the backyard. Her magical rebozo never left anyone out.

But after one fierce tug-of-war, Maya's *rebozo* ripped in two!

Así que, con sus propias manos y la ayuda de Abuelita, Maya convirtió la falda que había sido su vestido, que había sido su manta, en un rebozo que quería mucho. Maya se ponía el rebozo cuando jugaba con sus amigos en el patio. Su rebozo mágico nunca dejó a nadie fuera del juego.

Pero después de un intenso juego de tira y afloja, ¡el rebozo de Maya se desgarró!

So with her own two hands and Abuelita's help, Maya made her *rebozo* that was her *falda* that was her *vestido* that was her *manta* into a *bufanda* that she loved very much. She wore the scarf on cold, windy days. Her magical *bufanda* kept her from blowing away.

But after a couple of winters, Maya's *bufanda* was old and worn. It was falling apart before her eyes.

So with her own two hands and Abuelita's help, Maya made
her *cinta* that was her *bufanda* that was her *rebozo* that was her
falda that was her *vestido* that was her *manta* into a *marcador de
libros* that she loved very much. Maya always read before going to
bed, and at night her magical bookmark slept between the pages
of her favorite book.

Así que, con sus propias manos y la ayuda de Abuelita, Maya
convirtió su cinta que había sido su bufanda, que había sido su
rebozo, que había sido su falda, que había sido su vestido, que
había sido su manta, en un marcador de libros que quería mucho.
Maya siempre leía antes de acostarse y, de noche, su marcador
de libros mágico dormía entre las páginas de su libro favorito.

Así que, con sus propias manos y la ayuda de Abuelita, Maya convirtió
su bufanda que había sido su rebozo, que había sido su falda, que había
sido su vestido, que había sido su manta, en una cinta que quería mucho.
Maya usó la cinta mágica para recogerse el largo pelo castaño cuando
jugaba al fútbol. Su cinta mágica la ayudó a anotar varios ¡gooooooooooles!
Pero cuando Maya se cortó el pelo, ya no necesitó la cinta.

So with her own two hands and Abuelita's help, Maya made her *bufanda* that was her *rebozo* that was her *falda* that was her *vestido* that was her *manta* into a *cinta* that she loved very much. Maya wore the ribbon tied around her long, brown hair whenever she played soccer. Her magical *cinta* helped her score many goooooooooals!

But when Maya had her hair cut short, she didn't need a *cinta* anymore.

Así que, con sus propias manos y la ayuda de Abuelita, Maya convirtió el rebozo que había sido su falda, que había sido su vestido, que había sido su manta, en una bufanda que quería mucho. Maya usaba la bufanda durante los días fríos y ventosos. Su bufanda mágica no permitía que el viento se llevara a Maya.

Pero después de un par de inviernos, la bufanda de Maya estaba vieja y gastada. Maya notó que se comenzaba a hacer pedazos.

But one day Maya lost her *marcador de libros* that was her *cinta* that was her *bufanda* that was her *rebozo* that was her *falda* that was her *vestido* that was her *manta*. Maya was very sad. She looked everywhere, but the *marcador de libros* was nowhere to be found. Most of all, she missed the magic.

Maya didn't know what else to do, so she sat and thought. Then she had an idea!

Pero un día, Maya perdió su marcador de libros que había sido
su cinta, que había sido su bufanda, que había sido su rebozo,
que había sido su falda, que había sido su vestido, que había sido
su manta. Maya estaba muy triste. Lo buscó por todas partes,
pero no logró encontrarlo. Sobre todo, extrañaba la magia.

Maya no sabía qué hacer, así que se sentó a pensar. ¡Hasta que
tuvo una idea!

Maya made up a story about the *marcador de libros*, the *cinta*, the *bufanda*, the *rebozo*, the *falda*, and the *vestido* that had come from her beautiful blue-and-green *manta* with purple butterflies that Abuelita had stitched with her own two hands.

Maya remembered and wrote and drew all her adventures and made them into a *libro*. She called her book *Maya's Blanket/ La manta de Maya*, and she found magic on every page.

Maya creó una historia sobre el marcador de libros, la cinta, la bufanda, el rebozo, la falda y el vestido que salieron de la hermosa manta azul y verde con mariposas moradas que Abuelita le había cosido con sus propias manos.

Maya recordó y escribió y dibujó todas sus aventuras y las convirtió en un libro. Lo llamó *Maya's Blanket/La manta de Maya*, y allí encontró magia en cada página.

When Maya grew up, she had a little daughter whom she loved very much. Each night, after her daughter was in bed, Maya read to her.

Maya's daughter listened and laughed and snuggled . . .

Cuando Maya creció, tuvo una hijita que quería mucho.

Cada noche, antes de que se fuera a dormir, Maya le leía
en la cama.

La hija de Maya escuchaba y se reía y se acurrucaba…

. . . under her own special, magical *manta*.

...bajo su propia manta especial y mágica.

Author's Note

What if the objects we love—blankets, stuffed animals, dolls, toys—never leave us? Think creatively about how to recycle and reuse your favorite well-worn treasures. If they can't be reused in some kind of craft project, then recycle them using your imagination. Create a poem, a song, or even . . . your very own book!

Maya's Blanket/La manta de Maya was inspired by the traditional Yiddish folk song "Hob Ikh Mir a Mantl" ("I Had a Little Coat"), about an old overcoat that is continually repurposed as smaller and smaller items. "Hob Ikh Mir a Mantl" was written long before Earth Day came into being, but it celebrates both creativity and recycling.

In *Maya's Blanket/La manta de Maya*, I am also honoring both my Jewish and Latina heritage. I think of my mother tucking me in each night, telling me stories of her childhood in Peru as I snuggled under my yellow blanket decorated with orange butterflies. I also think of my nana, who, with infinite patience and love, taught me how to sew and embroider.

Glossary

Abuelita (ah-bweh-LEE-tah): Grandma

(la) bufanda (boo-FAHN-dah): scarf

(la) cinta (SEEN-tah): ribbon

(la) falda (FAHL-dah): skirt

(el) libro (LEE-broh): book

(la) manta (MAHN-tah): blanket

(el) marcador de libros (mahr-kah-DOHR deh LEE-brohs): bookmark

(la) quinceañera (keen-seh-ah-NYAI-rah): girl's fifteenth birthday celebration

(el) rebozo (reh-BOH-zoh): shawl

(el) vestido (bes-TEE-doh): dress

Nota de la autora

¿Que sucedería si los objetos que queremos —como las mantas, los animales de peluche, las muñecas y los juguetes— no nos dejaran nunca? Trata de buscar modos creativos de reciclar y reutilizar tus propios tesoros gastados. Si no lo haces cosiendo o con artesanías, puedes lograrlo con tu imaginación. Escribe un poema, una canción, o hasta…¡tu propio libro!

Maya's Blanket/La manta de Maya fue inspirada por la canción folklórica judía "Hob Ikh Mir a Mantl" ("Tenía un pequeño abrigo"), sobre un viejo abrigo que se reutiliza continuamente en forma de artículos cada vez más pequeños. "Hob Ikh Mir a Mantl" fue escrita mucho antes de que existiera el Día de la Tierra, pero aun así, celebraba el reciclaje y la creatividad.

Con *Maya's Blanket/La manta de Maya*, rindo homenaje a mis dos herencias culturales: la judía y la hispana. Recuerdo cuando mi mamá me arropaba bajo mi manta amarilla con mariposas anaranjadas mientras me contaba historias sobre su niñez en Perú. También recuerdo a mi nana, quien, con infinita paciencia y amor, me enseñó a coser y a bordar.